DRAGON KITES AND DRAGONFLIES

A COLLECTION
OF CHINESE NURSERY RHYMES

ADAPTED AND
ILLUSTRATED BY Demi

HARCOURT BRACE JOVANOVICH, PUBLISHERS

SAN DIEGO   NEW YORK   LONDON

Dragon Kites and Dragonflies

FOR VIRGINIA L. SWIFT, LIBRARIAN, CHATHAM SQUARE LIBRARY, CHINATOWN, NEW YORK CITY

—and for all her children

LIBRARY OF CONGRESS CATALOGING IN PUBLICATION DATA
Demi.
Dragon kites and dragonflies.
Summary: An illustrated collection of twenty-two traditional Chinese nursery rhymes.
1. Nursery rhymes, Chinese. 2. Children's poetry, Chinese.
[1. Nursery rhymes. 2. Chinese poetry] I. Title.
PZ8.3.D4314Dr 1986   398'.8   86-7637
ISBN 0-15-224199-X

J
398.8
Demi

Printed in the United States of America

FIRST EDITION   A B C D E

Some of the nursery rhymes in this book were given to Demi by Tze-Si "Jesse" Huang, who remembered them from his childhood in Wildcat Stream, Chungking, Szechuan, where he played with dragon boats, dragon kites, and sang some dragon songs. Others were adapted from *Chinese Mother Goose Rhymes*, translated by Isaac Taylor Headland (Fleming H. Revell Company, Westwood, New Jersey, 1900), and from *Chinese Children's Rhymes* by Ruth Hsu (The Commercial Press, Limited, Shanghai, 1935).

The choice of colors for this book was inspired by the magnificent cultural heritage of China. Dazzling paper kites, brilliant embroideries, unbelievable candy sculptures, and colorful rituals still performed, such as the dragon boat race and the Chinese wedding — once seen, they are forever held fast in memory.

The paintings in this book were done in watercolor.
The text type was set on the Linotron 202W in Cochin.
The display type was photoset in Zapf Chancery Demi.
Color separations were made by Heinz Weber, Inc., Los Angeles, California.
Composed by Adroit Graphic Composition Inc., New York, New York.
Printed by Holyoke Lithograph Co. Inc., Springfield, Massachusetts.
Bound by A. Horowitz and Sons, Bookbinders, Fairfield, New Jersey.
Production supervision by Warren Wallerstein.
Typography and binding design by Barbara DuPree Knowles.

Dragonfly, dragonfly,
Sailing freely in the sky,
Gliding on the summer breeze
Up and down as you please.

Flying alone, feeding in the sun,
Coming home when the day is done,
Free and happy in your heart.
Surely your life's a life apart.

This is baby's trumpet,
Toot! Toot! Too!
This is sister's shuttlecock,
Flying off her shoe.
This is baby's hammer,
Ding! Ding! Ding!
Look at all the painted kites
Humming on their strings!

Little baby, full of glee,
Won't you come and play with me?
Strike the bat and kick the ball,
And we will picnic by the wall.
And you shall come and eat with me,
And you shall come and drink my tea.
When I invite you thus to play,
How is it that you run away?

If you chance to be crossing
The camelback bridge,
Each step leads you up
Till you come to the ridge.

The lantern grass floats
On the pond like a sail.
The silver fish bites
At the goldfish's tail.

The placid green frog,
Sitting flat on a rock,
Keeps constantly calling,
"Whar-rah! Whar-rock!"

"Froggie, froggie,
  How old are you?"
"Just exactly twenty-two."
"Froggie, froggie,
  Where do you rest?"
"Big river east,
  Little river west,
  Among the green rushes
  In a mud nest."

The mighty Emperor Ch'in Shih Huang
Built a wall both great and strong;
It was so long and very stout
That it kept the dangerous Tartars out.

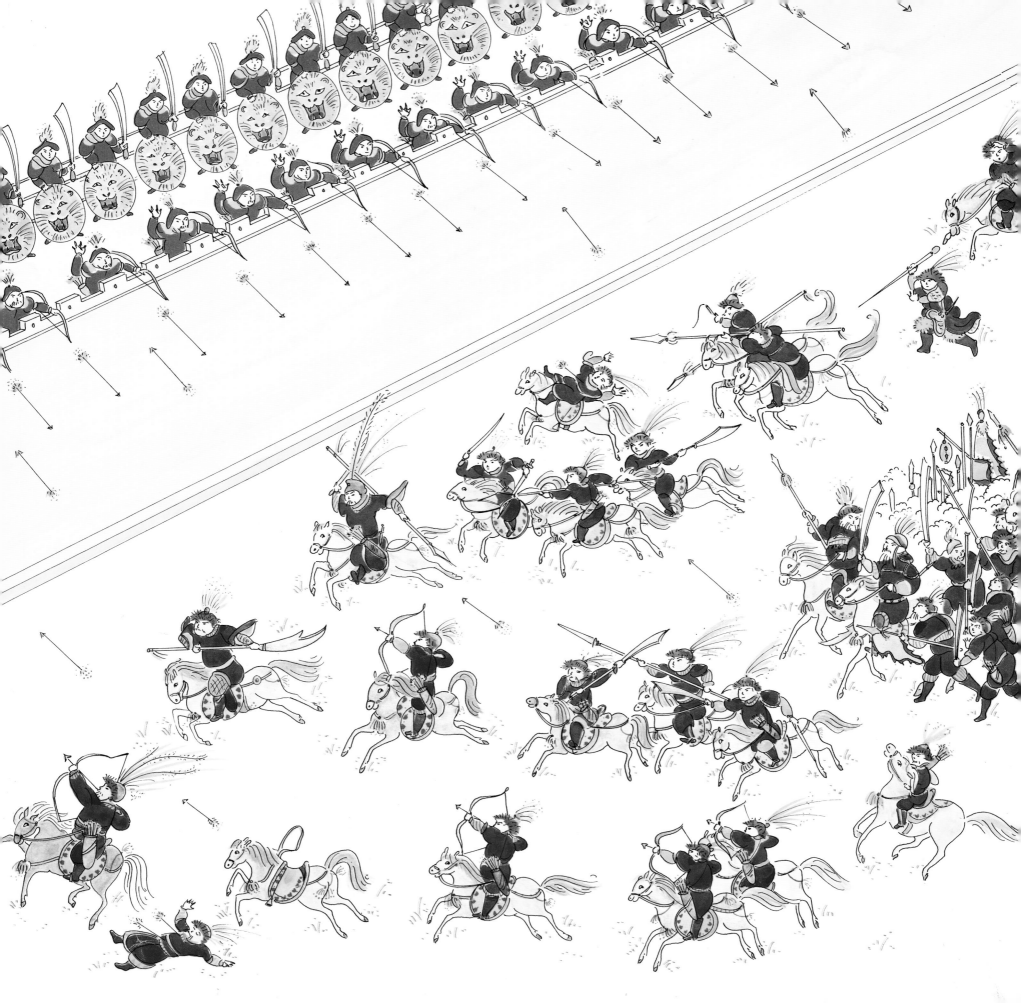

The dragon boats! There they go!
Beat the drums! Row and row!
The swiftest dragon in the race
Will be the dragon in first place!

The New Year lanterns
Are gay and entrancing.
Under their light
The children are dancing.

A peacock feather
On a plum-tree limb,
You catch me,
And I'll catch him!

A wee little boy has opened a store
A little away from his own front door.
A wee little table, a wee little chair,
Wee little chopsticks and a wee bowl are there.

Little silk worms, if you please,
Eat up all the mulberry leaves.
Make cocoons as white as milk,
And we'll make clothes of purest silk.

The acrobats are jumping around.
They can juggle a jar that weighs forty pounds.
They are able to do all kinds of tricks
With the hoop and the wheel or daggers and sticks.

Beat the drum, beat the drum!
The bride is carried in a chair.
Blow the horns, strike the gong!
Wave the banners in the air.
Rum pum pum! Beat the drum!
The groom's white horse is coming.
Clear the way! Clear the way!
Don't you hear the drumming?

The lazy woman
She sweeps the floor
And leaves the dirt
Inside the door.

She cooks her rice
In a dirty pot
And sleeps at night
On an old wood cot.

The tidy woman
Is always clean.
No dirt in her home
Is ever seen.

Her food is fit
For a king to eat,
And her hair and clothes
Are always neat.

The Moon King's knife of silver bright
Floats over the waves on a quiet night,
Floats to the fairy Southern Sea
Where grows the giant pepper tree.
When the pepper seeds to sea have gone,
The spring child sings his first little song.

The wild swan's call
Is heard from the skies.
When it is hungry
How sadly it cries;
But when it is satisfied,
It sings as it flies.

Fireflies, fireflies,
Tiny lanterns in the sky,
You fly up high,
You fly down low;
Now on sister's
Dress you glow.

Splashing water, lantern grass,
Children herding oxen pass
Right along the riverside.
Yes, the world is very wide!
Someone's singing very loud
To a lovely little cloud.

The day has come;
I hear the cock.
Get up and dress
It's six o'clock.

This little fellow was naughty, they say.
They sent him to watch the melons all day!

Put on your shoes and don't be late,
The puppets are playing at Grandmother's gate.
Big sisters and brothers run off to the show,
But all of us, even the baby, will go.